All That Matters
by
EDGAR A. GUEST

"All That Matters"
Is Dedicated
To My Wife
Who Is
All To Me

E. A. G.

ALL THAT MATTERS

When all that matters shall be written downAnd the long record of our years is told,Where sham, like flesh, must perish and grow cold;When the tomb closes on our fair renownAnd priest and layman, sage and motleyed clownMust quit the places which they dearly hold,What to our credit shall we find enscrolled?And what shall be the jewels of our crown?I fancy we shall hear to our surpriseSome little deeds of kindness, long forgot,Telling our glory, and the brave and wiseDeeds which we boasted often, mentioned not.God gave us life not just to buy and sell,And all that matters is to live it well.

UNTIL SHE DIED

Until she died we never knewThe beauty of our faith in God.We'd seen the summer roses nodAnd wither as the tempests blew,Through many a spring we'd lived to seeThe buds returning to the tree.

We had not felt the touch of woe;What cares had come, had lightly flown;Our burdens we had borne alone—The need of God we did not know.It seemed sufficient through the daysTo think and act in worldly ways.

And then she closed her eyes in sleep;She left us for a little while;No more our lives would know her smile.And oh, the hurt of it went deep!It seemed to us that we must fallBefore the anguish of it all.

Our faith, which had not known the test,Then blossomed with its comfort sweet,Promised that some day we should meetAnd whispered to us: "He knows best."And when our bitter tears were dried,We found our faith was glorified.

THE CALL

I must get out to the woods again, to the whispering tree, and the birds a-wing,Away from the haunts of pale-faced men, to the spaces wide where strength is king;I must get out where the skies are blue and the air is clean and the rest is sweet,Out where there's never a task to do or a goal to reach or a foe to meet.

I must get out on the trails once more that wind through shadowy haunts and cool,Away from the presence of wall and door, and see myself in a crystal pool;I must get out with the silent things, where neither laughter nor hate is heard,Where malice never the humblest stings and no one is hurt by a spoken word.

Oh, I've heard the call of the tall white pine, and heard the call of the running brook;I'm tired of the tasks which each day are mine, I'm weary of reading a printed book;I want to get out of the din and strife, the clang and clamor of turning wheel,And walk for a day where life is life, and the joys are true and the pictures real.

[Pg 12]

MOTHER AND THE BABY

Mother and the baby! Oh, I know no lovelier pair,For all the dreams of all the world are hovering 'round them there;And be the baby in his cot or nestling in her arms,The picture they present is one with never-fading charms.

Mother and the baby—and the mother's eye aglowWith joys that only mothers see and only mothers know!And here is all there is to strife and all there is to fame,And all that men have struggled for since first a baby came.

I never see this lovely pair nor hear the mother singThe lullabies of babyhood, but I start wonderingHow much of every man to-day the world thinks wise or braveIs of the songs his mother sang and of the strength she gave.

"Mother And The Baby"
From a drawing by **W. T. BENDA.**

"Just like a mother!" Oh, to be so tender and so true,No man has reached so high a plane with all he's dared to do.[Pg 13]And yet, I think she understands, with every step she takesAnd every care that she bestows, it is the man she makes.

Mother and the baby! And in fancy I can seeHer life being given gladly to the man that is to be,And from her strength and sacrifice and from her lullabies,She dreams and hopes and nightly prays a strong man shall arise.

[Pg 14]

OLD-FASHIONED LETTERS

Old-fashioned letters! How good they were!And nobody writes them now;Never at all comes in the scrawlOn the written pages which told us allThe news of town and the folks we knew,And what they had done or were going to do.It seems we've forgotten howTo spend an hour with our pen in handTo write in the language we understand.

Old-fashioned letters we used to getAnd ponder each fond line o'er;The glad words rolled like running gold,As smoothly their tales of joy they told,And our hearts beat fast with a keen delightAs we read the news they were pleased to writeAnd gathered the love they bore.But few of the letters that come to-dayAre penned to us in the old-time way.

Old-fashioned letters that told us all The tales of the far away; Where they'd been and the folks they'd seen; And better than any fine magazine Was the writing too, for it bore the style Of a simple heart and a sunny smile, And was pure as the breath of May. Some of them oft were damp with tears, But those were the letters that lived for years. [Pg 15]

Old-fashioned letters! How good they were! And, oh, how we watched the mails; But nobody writes of the quaint delights Of the sunny days and the merry nights Or tells us the things that we yearn to know—That art passed out with the long ago, And lost are the simple tales; Yet we all would happier be, I think, If we'd spend more time with our pen and ink.

[Pg 16]

GOD MADE THIS DAY FOR ME

Jes' the sort o' weather and jes' the sort o' sky Which seem to suit my fancy, with the white clouds driftin' by On a sea o' smooth blue water. Oh, I ain't an egotist, With an "I" in all my thinkin', but I'm willin' to insist That the Lord that made us humans an' the birds in every tree Knows my special sort o' weather an' He made this day fer me.

This is jes' my style o' weather—sunshine floodin' all the place, An' the breezes from the eastward blowin' gently on my face. An' the woods chock-full o' singin' till you'd think birds never had A single care to fret 'em or a grief to make 'em sad. Oh, I settle down contented in the shadow of a tree, An' tell myself right proudly that the day was made fer me.

"God Made This Day For Me"
From a painting by **M. L. BOWER.**

[Pg 17]

It's my day, sky an' sunshine, an' the temper o' the breeze. Here's the weather I would fashion could I run things as I please—Beauty dancin' all around me, music ringin' everywhere, Like a weddin' celebration. Why, I've plumb fergot my care An' the tasks I should be doin' fer the rainy days to be, While I'm huggin' the delusion that God made this day fer me.

[Pg 18]

FORGETFUL PA

My Pa says that he used to be A bright boy in geography; An' when he went to school he knew The rivers an' the mountains, too, An' all the capitals of states An' bound'ry lines an' all the dates They joined the union. But last night When I was studyin' to recite I asked him if he would explain The leading industries of Maine—He thought an' thought an' thought a lot, An' said, "I knew, but I've forgot."

My Pa says when he was in school He got a hundred as a rule; An' grammar was a thing he knew Becoz he paid attention to His teacher, an' he learned the way To write good English, an' to say The proper things, an' I should be As good a boy in school as he. But once

I asked him could he giveMe help with the infinitive—He scratched his head and said: "Great Scott!I used to know, but I've forgot."[Pg 19]

My Pa says when he was a boyArithmetic was just a toy;He learned his tables mighty fastAn' every term he always passed,An' had good marks, an' teachers said:"That youngster surely has a head."But just the same I notice nowMost every time I ask him howTo find the common multiple,He says, "That's most unusual!Once I'd have told you on the spot,But somehow, sonny, I've forgot."I'm tellin' you just what is what,My Pa's forgot an awful lot!

[Pg 20]

MOTHERHOOD

I wonder if he'll stop to think,When the long years have traveled by,Who heard his plea: "I want a drink!"Who was the first to hear him cry?I wonder if he will recallThe patience of her and the smile,The kisses after every fall,The love that lasted all the while?

I wonder, as I watch them there,If he'll remember, when he's grown,How came the silver in her hairAnd why her loveliness has flown?Yet thus my mother did for me,Night after night and day by day,For such a care I used to be,As such a boy I used to play.

I know that I was always sureOf tenderness at mother's knee,That every hurt of mine she'd cure,And every fault she'd fail to see.But who recalls the tears she shed,And all the wishes gratified,The eager journeys to his bed,The pleas which never she denied?

"Motherhood"
From a painting by ROBERT E. JOHNSTON.

[Pg 21]

I took for granted, just as he,The boundless love that mother gives,But watching them I've come to seeTime teaches every man who livesHow much of him is not his own;And now I know the countless waysBy which her love for me was shown,And I recall forgotten days.

Perhaps some day a little chapAs like him as he's now like me,Shall climb into his mother's lap,For comfort and for sympathy,And he shall know what now I know,And see through eyes a trifle dim,The mother of the long agoWho daily spent her strength for him.

[Pg 22]

PLAYING FOR KEEPS

I've watched him change from his bibs and things, from bonnets known as "cute,"To little frocks, and later on I saw him don a suit;And though it was of calico, those knickers gave him joy,Until the day we all agreed 'twas time for corduroy.I say I've seen the changes come, it seems with bounds and leaps,But here's another just arrived—he's playing mibs for keeps!

The guide posts of his life fly by. The boy that is to-day,To-morrow morning we may wake to find has gone away,And in his place will be a lad we've never known before,Older and wiser in his ways, and filled with new-found lore.Now here's another boy to-day, counting his marble heapsAnd proudly boasting to his dad he's playing mibs for keeps!

His mother doesn't like this change. She says it is a shame—That since he plays with larger boys, he's bound to lose the game.[Pg 23]But little do I mind his loss; I'm more concerned to knowThe way he acts the times when he must see his marbles go.And oh, I hope he will not be the little boy who weepsToo much when he has failed to win while playing mibs for keeps.

Playing for keeps! Another step toward manhood's broad estate!This is what some term growing up, or destiny, or fate.Yet from this game with marbles, played with youngsters on the street,I hope will come a larger boy, too big to lie or cheat,And by these mibs which from his clutch another madly sweeps,I hope he'll learn the game of life which must be played for keeps.

[Pg 24]
THE FROSTING DISH

When I was just a little tadNot more than eight or nine,One special treat to make me gladWas set apart as "mine."On baking days she granted meThe small boy's dearest wish,And when the cake was finished, sheGave me the frosting dish.

I've eaten chocolate many ways,I've had it hot and cold;I've sampled it throughout my daysIn every form it's sold.And though I still am fond of it,And hold its flavor sweet,The icing dish, I still admit,Remains the greatest treat.

Never has chocolate tasted so,Nor brought to me such joyAs in those days of long agoWhen I was but a boy,And stood beside my mother fair,Waiting the time when sheWould gently stoop to kiss me thereAnd hand the plate to me.

"The Frosting Dish"
From a painting by H. C. PITZ.

[Pg 25]
Now there's another in my placeWho stands where once I stood.And watches with an upturned faceAnd waits for "something good."And as she hands him spoon and plateI chuckle low and wishThat I might be allowed to waitTo scrape the frosting dish.

[Pg 26]
PLAY THE GAME

When the umpire calls you out,It's no use to stamp and shout,Wildly kicking dust about—Play the game!And though his decision mayEnd your chances for the day,Rallies often end that way—Play the game!

When the umpire shouts: "Strike two!"And the ball seems wide to you,There is just one thing to do:Play the game!Keep your temper at the plate,Grit your teeth and calmly wait,For the next one may be straightPlay the game!

When you think the umpire's wrong,Tell him so, but jog along;Nothing's gained by language strong—Play the game!For his will must be obeyedWheresoever baseball's played,Take his verdict as it's made—Play the game![Pg 27]

Son of mine, beyond a doubt,Fate shall often call you "out,"But keep on, with courage stout—Play the game!In the battlefield of menThere'll come trying moments whenYou shall lose the verdict—thenPlay the game!

There's an umpire who shall sayYou have missed your greatest play,And shall dash your hopes away—Play the game!You must bow unto his willThough your chance it seems to kill,And you think he erred, but stillPlay the game!

For the Great Umpire aboveSees what we see nothing of,By His wisdom and His love—Play the game!Keep your faith in Him althoughHis grim verdicts hurt you so,At His Will we come and go—Play the game!

[Pg 28]

WHEN THE YOUNG ARE GROWN

Once the house was lovely, but it's lonely here to-day,For time has come an' stained its walls an' called the young away;An' all that's left for mother an' for me till life is throughIs to sit an' tell each other what the children used to do.

We couldn't keep 'em always an' we knew it from the start;We knew when they were babies that some day we'd have to part.But the years go by so swiftly, an' the littlest one has flown,An' there's only me an' mother now left here to live alone.

Oh, there's just one consolation, as we're sittin' here at night,They've grown to men an' women, an' we brought 'em up all right;We've watched 'em as we've loved 'em an' they're splendid, every one,An' we feel the Lord won't blame us for the way our work was done.

"When The Young Are Grown"
From a painting by **ROBERT E. JOHNSTON.**

[Pg 29]

They're clean, an' kind an' honest, an' the world respects 'em, too;That's the dream of parents always, an' our dreams have all come true.So although the house is lonely an' sometimes our eyes grow wet,We are proud of them an' happy an' we've nothing to regret.

[Pg 30]

THE BOY'S IDEAL

I must be fit for a child to play with,Fit for a youngster to walk away with;Fit for his trust and fit to beReady to take him upon my knee;Whether I win or I lose my fight,I must be fit for my boy at night.

I must be fit for a child to come to,Speech there is that I must be dumb to;I must be fit for his eyes to see,He must find nothing of shame in me;Whatever I make of myself, I mustSquare to my boy's unfaltering trust.

I must be fit for a child to follow,Scorning the places where loose men wallow;Knowing how much he shall learn from me,I must be fair as I'd have him be;I must come home to him, day by day,Clean as the morning I went away.

I must be fit for a child's glad greeting,His are eyes that there is no cheating;He must behold me in every test,Not at my worst, but my very best;He must be proud when my life is doneTo have men know that he is my son.

[Pg 31]

JUST HALF OF THAT, PLEASE

Grandmother says when I pass her the cake:"Just half of that, please."If I serve her the tenderest portion of steak:"Just half of that, please."And be the dessert a rice pudding or pie,As I pass Grandma's share she is sure to reply,With the trace of a twinkle to light up her eye:"Just half of that, please."

I've cut down her portions but still she tells me:"Just half of that, please."Though scarcely a mouthful of food she can see:"Just half of that, please."If I pass her the chocolates she breaks one in two,There's nothing so small but a smaller will do,And she says, perhaps fearing she's taking from you:"Just half of that, please."

When at last Grandma leaves us the angels will hear:"Just half of that, please."When with joys for the gentle and brave they appear:"Just half of that, please."And for fear they may think she is selfish up there,Or is taking what may be a young angel's share,She will say with the loveliest smile she can wear:"Just half of that, please."

[Pg 32]

THE COMMON TOUCH

I would not be too wise—so very wiseThat I must sneer at simple songs and creeds,And let the glare of wisdom blind my eyesTo humble people and their humble needs.

I would not care to climb so high that ICould never hear the children at their play,Could only see the people passing by,Yet never hear the cheering words they say.

I would not know too much—too much to smileAt trivial errors of the heart and hand,Nor be too proud to play the friend the while,And cease to help and know and understand.

I would not care to sit upon a throne,Or build my house upon a mountain-top,Where I must dwell in glory all aloneAnd never friend come in or poor man stop.

God grant that I may live upon this earthAnd face the tasks which every morning brings,And never lose the glory and the worthOf humble service and the simple things.

"The Common Touch"
From a painting by HARVEY EMRICH.

[Pg 33]

MARJORIE

The house is as it was when she was here;There's nothing changed at all about the place;The books she loved to read are waiting nearAs if to-morrow they would see her face;Her room remains the way it used to be,Here are the puzzles that she pondered on:Yet since the angels called for MarjorieThe joyous spirit of the home has gone.

All things grew lovely underneath her touch,The room was bright because it knew her smile;From her the tiniest trinket gathered much,The cheapest toy became a thing worth while;Yet here are her possessions as they were,No longer joys to set the eyes aglow;To-day, as we, they seem to mourn for her,And share the sadness that is ours to know.

Half sobbing now, we put her games away,Because, dumb things, they cannot understandWhy never more shall Marjorie come to play,And we have faith in God at our command.These toys we smiled at once, now start our tears,They seem to wonder why they lie so still,They call her name, and will throughout the years—God, strengthen us to bow unto Thy will.

[Pg 34]

THE NEWSPAPER MAN

Bit of a priest and a bit of sailor,Bit of a doctor and bit of a tailor,Bit of a lawyer, and bit of detective,Bit of a judge, for his work is corrective;Cheering the living and soothing the dying,Risking all things, even dare-devil flying;True to his paper and true to his clan—Just look him over, the newspaper man.

Sleep! There are times that he'll do with a little,Work till his nerves and his temper are brittle;Fire cannot daunt him, nor long hours disturb him,Gold cannot buy him and threats cannot curb him;Highbrow or lowbrow, your own speech he'll hand you,Talk as you will to him, he'll understand you;He'll go wherever another man can—That is the way of the newspaper man.

Surgeon, if urgent the need be, you'll find him,Ready to help, nor will dizziness blind him;He'll give the ether and never once falter,Say the last rites like a priest at the altar;Gentle and kind with the weak and the weary,Which is proved now and then when his keen eye grows teary;Facing all things in life's curious plan—That is the way of the newspaper man.[Pg 35]

One night a week may he rest from his labor,One night at home to be father and neighbor;Just a few hours for his own bit of leisure,All the rest's gazing at other men's pleasure,All the rest's toiling, and yet he rejoices,All the world is, and that men do, he voices—Who knows a calling more glorious thanThe day-by-day work of the newspaper man?

[Pg 36]
A BOY AND HIS DAD

A boy and his dad on a fishing-trip—There is a glorious fellowship!Father and son and the open skyAnd the white clouds lazily drifting by,And the laughing stream as it runs alongWith the clicking reel like a martial song,And the father teaching the youngster gayHow to land a fish in the sportsman's way.

I fancy I hear them talking thereIn an open boat, and the speech is fair.And the boy is learning the ways of menFrom the finest man in his youthful ken.Kings, to the youngster, cannot compareWith the gentle father who's with him there.And the greatest mind of the human raceNot for one minute could take his place.

Which is happier, man or boy?The soul of the father is steeped in joy,For he's finding out, to his heart's delight,That his son is fit for the future fight.He is learning the glorious depths of him,And the thoughts he thinks and his every whim;And he shall discover, when night comes on,How close he has grown to his little son.

"A Boy And His Dad"
From a painting by **M. L. BOWER.**

[Pg 37]
A boy and his dad on a fishing-trip—Builders of life's companionship!Oh, I envy them, as I see them thereUnder the sky in the open air,For out of the old, old long-agoCome the summer days that I used to know,When I learned life's truths from my father's lipsAs I shared the joy of his fishing-trips.

[Pg 38]
BREAD AND GRAVY

There's a heap o' satisfaction in a chunk o' pumpkin pie,An' I'm always glad I'm livin' when the cake is passin' by;An' I guess at every meal-time I'm as happy as can be,For I like whatever dishes Mother gets for Bud an' me;But there's just one bit of eatin' which I hold supremely great,An' that's good old bread and gravy when I've finished up my plate.

I've eaten fancy dishes an' my mouth has watered, too;I've been at banquet tables an' I've run the good things through;I've had sea food up in Boston, I've had pompano down South,For most everything that's edible I've put into my mouth;But the finest treat I know of, now I publicly relate,Is a chunk of bread and gravy when I've finished up my plate.

Now the epicures may snicker and the hotel chefs may smile,But when it comes to eating I don't hunger much for style;[Pg 39]For an empty man wants fillin' an' you can't do that with thingsLike breast o' guinea under glass, or curried turkey wings—You want just plain home cookin' an' the chance to sit an' waitFor a piece o' bread an' gravy when you've finished up your plate.

Oh, it may be I am common an' my tastes not much refined,But the meals which suit my fancy are the good old-fashioned kind,With the food right on the table an' the hungry kids aboutAn' the mother an' the father handing all the good things out,An' the knowledge in their presence that I needn't fear to state,That I'd like some bread an' gravy when I've finished up my plate.

[Pg 40]

THE GRATE FIRE

I'm sorry for a fellow if he cannot look and seeIn a grate fire's friendly flaming all the joys which used to be.If in quiet contemplation of a cheerful ruddy blazeHe sees nothing there recalling all his happy yesterdays,Then his mind is dead to fancy and his life is bleak and bare,And he's doomed to walk the highways that are always thick with care.

When the logs are dry as tinder and they crackle with the heat,And the sparks, like merry children, come a-dancing round my feet,In the cold, long nights of autumn I can sit before the blazeAnd watch a panorama born of all my yesterdays.I can leave the present burdens and that moment's bit of woe,And claim once more the gladness of the bygone long ago.

"The Grate Fire"
From a drawing by **W. T. BENDA.**

There are no absent faces in the grate fire's merry throng;No hands in death are folded, and no lips are stilled to song.All the friends who were are living—like the sparks that fly about;[Pg 41]They come romping out to greet me with the same old merry shout,Till it seems to me I'm playing once again on boyhood's stage,Where there's no such thing as sorrow and there's no such thing as age.

I can be the care-free schoolboy! I can play the lover, too!I can walk through Maytime orchards with the old sweetheart I knew;I can dream the glad dreams over, greet the old familiar friendsIn a land where there's no parting and the laughter never ends.All the gladness life has given from a grate fire I reclaim,And I'm sorry for the fellow who can only see the flame.

[Pg 42]

THE KINDLY NEIGHBOR

I have a kindly neighbor, one who standsBeside my gate and chats with me awhile,Gives me the glory of his radiant smileAnd comes at times to help with willing hands.No station high or rank this man commands,He, too, must trudge, as I, the long day's mile;And yet, devoid of pomp or gaudy style,He has a worth exceeding stocks or lands.

To him I go when sorrow's at my door,On him I lean when burdens come my way,Together oft we talk our trials o'erAnd there is warmth in each good-night we say.A kindly neighbor! Wars and strife shall endWhen man has made the man next door his friend.

[Pg 43]
THE TEARS EXPRESSIVE
Death crossed his threshold yesterdayAnd left the glad voice of his loved one dumb.To him the living now will comeAnd cross his threshold in the self-same wayTo clasp his hand and vainly try to sayWords that shall soothe the heart that's stricken numb.

And I shall be among them in that placeSo still and silent, where she used to sing—The glad, sweet spirit that has taken wing—Where shone the radiance of her lovely face,And where she met him oft with fond embrace,I shall step in to share his sorrowing.

Beside the staircase that has known her handAnd in the hall her presence made complete,The home her life endowed with memories sweetWhere everything has heard her sweet commandAnd seems to wear her beauty, I shall standWondering just how to greet him when we meet.

I dread the very silence of the place,I dread our meeting and the time to speak—Speech seems so vain when sorrow's at the peak!Yet though my words lack soothing power or grace,Perhaps he'll catch their meaning in my faceAnd read the tears which glisten on my cheek.

[Pg 44]
THE JOYS WE MISS
There never comes a lonely day but what we miss the laughing waysOf those who used to walk with us through all our happy yesterdays.We seldom miss the earthly great—the famous men that life has known—But, as the years go racing by, we miss the friends we used to own.

The chair wherein he used to sit recalls the kindly father true,For, oh, so filled with fun he was, and, oh, so very much he knew!And as we face the problems grave with which the years of life are filled,We miss the hand which guided us and miss the voice forever stilled.

We little guessed how much he did to smooth our pathway day by day,How much of joy he brought to us, how much of care he brushed away;But now that we must tread alone the thoroughfare of life, we findHow many burdens we were spared by him who was so brave and kind.

"The Joys We Miss"
From a painting by **M. L. BOWER.**

[Pg 45]

Death robs the living, not the dead—they sweetly sleep whose tasks are done;But we are weaker than before who still must live and labor on.For when come care and grief to us, and heavy burdens bring us woe,We miss the smiling, helpful friends on whom we leaned long years ago.

We miss the happy, tender ways of those who brought us mirth and cheer;We never gather round the hearth but what we wish our friends were near;For peace is born of simple things—a kindly word, a good-night kiss,The prattle of a babe, and love—these are the vanished joys we miss.

[Pg 46]

LITTLE FEET

There is no music quite so sweetAs patter of a baby's feet.Who never hears along the hallThe sound of tiny feet that fallUpon the floor so soft and lowAs eagerly they come or go,Has missed, no matter who he be,Life's most inspiring symphony.

There is a music of the spheresToo fine to ring in mortal ears,Yet not more delicate and sweetThan pattering of baby feet;Where'er I hear that pit-a-patWhich falls upon the velvet mat,Out of my dreamy nap I startAnd hear the echo in my heart.

'Tis difficult to put in wordsThe music of the summer birds,Yet far more difficult a thing—A lyric for that pattering;Here is a music telling meOf golden joys that are to be;Unheralded by horns and drums,To me a regal caller comes.[Pg 47]

Now on my couch I lie and hearA little toddler coming near,Coming right boldly to my placeTo pull my hair and pat my face,Undaunted by my age or size,Nor caring that I am not wise—A visitor devoid of shamWho loves me just for what I am.

This soft low music tells to meIn just a minute I shall beMade captive by a thousand charms,Held fast by chubby little arms,For there is one upon the wayWho thinks the world was made for play.Oh, where's the sound that's half so sweetAs pattering of baby feet?

[Pg 48]

JUST LIKE A MAN

This is the phrase they love to say:"Just like a man!"You can hear it wherever you chance to stray:"Just like a man!"The wife of the toiler, the queen of the king,The bride with the shiny new wedding-ringAnd the grandmothers, too, at our sex will fling,"Just like a man!"

Cranky and peevish at times we grow:"Just like a man!"Now and then boastful of what we know:"Just like a man!"Whatever our failings from day to day—Stingy, or giving our goods away—With a toss of her head, she is sure to say,"Just like a man!"

Unannounced strangers we bring to tea:"Just like a man!"Heedless of every propriety:"Just like a man!"Grumbling at money she spends for spatsAnd filmy dresses and gloves and hats,Yet wanting her stylishly garbed, and that's"Just like a man!"

"Just Like A Man"
From a charcoal drawing by W. T. BENDA.

[Pg 49]
Wanting attention from year to year:"Just like a man!"Seemingly helpless when she's not near:"Just like a man!"Troublesome often, and quick to demur,Still remaining the boys we were,Yet soothed and blest by the love of her:"Just like a man!"

[Pg 50]

CLINCHING THE BOLT

It needed just an extra turn to make the bolt secure,A few more minutes on the job and then the work was sure;But he begrudged the extra turn, and when the task was through,The man was back for more repairs in just a day or two.

Two men there are in every place, and one is only fair,The other gives the extra turn to every bolt that's there;One man is slip-shod in his work and eager to be quit,The other never leaves a task until he's sure of it.

The difference 'twixt good and bad is not so very much,A few more minutes at the task, an extra turn or touch,A final test that all is right—and yet the men are fewWho seem to think it worth their while these extra things to do.[Pg 51]

The poor man knows as well as does the good man how to work,But one takes pride in every task, the other likes to shirk;With just as little as he can, one seeks his pay to earn,The good man always gives the bolt that clinching, extra turn.

[Pg 52]

HIS PA

Some fellers' pas seem awful old,An' talk like they was going to scold,An' their hair's all gone, an' they never grinOr holler an' shout when they come in.They don't get out in the street an' playThe way mine does at the close of day.It's just as funny as it can be,But my pa doesn't seem old to me.

He doesn't look old, an' he throws a ball,Just like a boy, with the curves an' all,An' he knows the kids by their first names, too,An' says they're just like the boys he knew.Some of the fellers are scared plumb stiffWhen their fathers are near 'em an' act as ifThey wuz doing wrong if they made a noise,But my pa seems to be one of the boys.

It's funny, but, somehow, I never canThink of my pa as a grown-up man.He doesn't frown an' he doesn't scold,An' he doesn't act as though he wuz old.He talks of the things I want to know,Just like one of our gang, an' so,Whenever we're out, it seems that heIs more like a pal than a pa to me.

"His Pa"
From a painting by M. L. BOWER.

[Pg 53]

EXAMPLE

Perhaps the victory shall not come to me,Perhaps I shall not reach the goal I seek,It may be at the last I shall be weakAnd falter as the promised land I see;Yet I must try for it and strive to beAll that a conqueror is. On to the peak,Must be my call—this way lies victory!Boy, take my hand and hear me when I speak.

There is the goal. In honor make the fight.I may not reach it but, my boy, you can.Cling to your faith and work with all your might,Some day the world shall hail you as a man.And when at last shall come your happy day,Enough for me that I have shown the way.

[Pg 54]

WINDING THE CLOCK

When I was but a little lad, my old Grandfather saidThat none should wind the clock but he, and so, at time for bed,He'd fumble for the curious key kept high upon the shelfAnd set aside that little task entirely for himself.

In time Grandfather passed away, and so that duty fellUnto my Father, who performed the weekly custom well;He held that clocks were not to be by careless persons wound,And he alone should turn the key or move the hands around.

I envied him that little task, and wished that I might beThe one to be entrusted with the turning of the key;But year by year the clock was his exclusive bit of careUntil the day the angels came and smoothed his silver hair.[Pg 55]

To-day the task is mine to do, like those who've gone beforeI am a jealous guardian of that round and glassy door,And 'til at my chamber door God's messenger shall knockTo me alone shall be reserved the right to wind the clock.

[Pg 56]

THE NEED

We were settin' there an' smokin' of our pipes, discussin' things,Like licker, votes for wimmin, an' the totterin' thrones o' kings,When he ups an' strokes his whiskers with his hand an' says t' me:"Changin' laws an' legislatures ain't, as fur as I can see,Goin' to make this world much better, unless somehow we canFind a way to make a better an' a finer sort o' man.

"The trouble ain't with statutes or with systems—not at all;It's with humans jus' like we air an' their petty ways an' small.We could stop our writin' law-books an' our regulatin' rulesIf a better sort of manhood was the product of our schools.For the things that we air needin' isn't writin' from a penOr bigger guns to shoot with, but a bigger type of men.

"The Need"
From a painting by PRUETT CARTER.

"I reckon all these problems air jest ornery like the weeds.They grow in soil that oughta nourish only decent deeds,[Pg 57]An' they waste our time an' fret us when, if we were thinkin' straightAn' livin' right, they wouldn't be so terrible and great.A good horse needs no snaffle, an' a good man, I opine,Doesn't need a law to check him or to force him into line.

"If we ever start in teachin' to our children, year by year,How to live with one another, there'll be less o' trouble here.If we'd teach 'em how to neighbor an' to walk in honor's ways,We could settle every problem which the mind o' man can raise.What we're needin' isn't systems or some regulatin' plan,But a bigger an' a finer an' a truer type o' man."

[Pg 58]
TEN-FINGERED MICE

When a cake is nicely frosted and it's put away for tea,And it looks as trim and proper as a chocolate cake should be,Would it puzzle you at evening as you brought it from the ledgeTo find the chocolate missing from its smooth and shiny edge?

As you viewed the cake in sorrow would you look around and say,"Who's been nibbling in the pantry when he should have been at play?"And if little eyes look guilty as they hungered for a slice,Would you take Dad's explanation that it must have been the mice?

Oh, I'm sorry for the household that can keep a frosted cakeSmooth and perfect through the daytime, for the hearts of them must ache—For it must be very lonely to be living in a houseWhere the pantry's never ravaged by a glad ten-fingered mouse.[Pg 59]

Though I've traveled far past forty, I confess that I, myself,Even now will nip a morsel from the good things on the shelf;And I never blame the youngsters who discover chocolate cakeFor the tiny little samples which exultantly they take.

[Pg 60]
THE THINGS
THEY MUSTN'T TOUCH

Been down to the art museum an' looked at a thousand things,The bodies of ancient mummies an' the treasures of ancient kings,An' some of the walls were lovely, but some of the things weren't much,But all had a rail around 'em, an' all wore a sign "Don't touch."

Now maybe an art museum needs guards and a warning signAn' the hands of the folks should never paw over its treasures fine;But I noticed the rooms were chilly with all the joys they hold,An' in spite of the lovely pictures, I'd say that the place is cold.

An' somehow I got to thinkin' of many a home I knowWhich is kept like an art museum, an' merely a place for show;They haven't railed off their treasures or posted up signs or such,But all of the children know it—there's a lot that they mustn't touch.[Pg 61]

It's hands off the grand piano, keep out of the finest chair,Stay out of the stylish parlor, don't run on the shiny stair;You may look at the velvet curtains which hang in the stately hall,But always and ever remember, they're not to be touched at all.

"Don't touch!" for an art museum, is proper enough, I know,But my children's feet shall scamper wherever they want to go,And I want no rare possessions or a joy which has cost so much,From which I must bar the children and tell them they "mustn't touch."

[Pg 62]

THE HARDER PART

It's mighty hard for Mother—I am busy through the dayAnd the tasks of every morning keep the gloomy thoughts away,And I'm not forever meeting with a slipper or a gownTo remind me of our sorrow when I'm toiling in the town.But with Mother it is different—there's no minute she is freeFrom the sight of things which tell her of the joy which used to be.

She is brave and she is faithful, and we say we're reconciled,But your hearts are always heavy once you've lost a little child;And a man can face his sorrow in a manly sort of way,For his grief must quickly leave him when he's busy through the day;But the mother's lot is harder—she must learn to sing and smileThough she's living in the presence of her sorrow all the while.

Through the room where love once waited she must tip-toe day by day,She must see through every window where the baby used to play,[Pg 63]And there's not a thing she touches, nor a task she finds to do,But it sets her heart to aching and begins the hurt anew.Oh, a man can turn from sorrow, for his mind is occupied,But the mother's lot is harder—grief is always at her side.

[Pg 64]

YOUTH

If I had youth I'd bid the world to try me;I'd answer every challenge to my will.Though mountains stood in silence to defy me,I'd try to make them subject to my skill.I'd keep my dreams and follow where they led me;I'd glory in the hazards which abound.I'd eat the simple fare privations fed me,And gladly make my couch upon the ground.

If I had youth I'd ask no odds of distance,Nor wish to tread the known and level ways.I'd want to meet and master strong resistance,And in a worth-while struggle spend my days.I'd seek the task which calls for full endeavor;I'd feel the thrill of battle in my veins.I'd bear my burden gallantly, and neverDesert the hills to walk on common plains.

If I had youth no thought of failure lurkingBeyond to-morrow's dawn should fright my soul.Let failure strike—it still should find me workingWith faith that I should some day reach my goal.I'd dice with danger—aye!—and glory in it;I'd make high stakes the purpose of my throw.I'd risk for much, and should I fail to win it,I would not even whimper at the blow.

"Youth"
From a drawing by W. T. BENDA.

[Pg 65]

If I had youth no chains of fear should bind me;I'd brave the heights which older men must shun.I'd leave the well-worn lanes of life behind me,And seek to do what men have never done.Rich prizes wait for those who do not waver;The world needs men to battle for the truth.It calls each hour for stronger hearts and braver.This is the age for those who still have youth!

[Pg 66]

ACCOMPLISHED CARE

All things grow lovely in a little while,The brush of memory paints a canvas fair;The dead face through the ages wears a smile,And glorious becomes accomplished care.

There's nothing ugly that can live for long,There's nothing constant in the realm of pain;Right always comes to take the place of wrong,Who suffers much shall find the greater gain.

Life has a kindly way, despite its tearsAnd all the burdens which its children bear;It crowns with beauty all the troubled yearsAnd soothes the hurts and makes their memory fair.

Be brave when days are bitter with despair,Be true when you are made to suffer wrong;Life's greatest joy is an accomplished care,There's nothing ugly that can live for long.

[Pg 67]

BULB PLANTING TIME

Last night he said the dead were deadAnd scoffed my faith to scorn;I found him at a tulip bedWhen I passed by at morn.

"O ho!" said I, "the frost is near.And mist is on the hills,And yet I find you planting hereTulips and daffodils."

"'Tis time to plant them now," he said,"If they shall bloom in Spring";"But every bulb," said I, "seems dead,And such an ugly thing."

"The pulse of life I cannot feel,The skin is dried and brown.Now look!" a bulb beneath my heelI crushed and trampled down.

In anger then he said to me:"You've killed a lovely thing;A scarlet blossom that would beSome morning in the Spring."

"Last night a greater sin was thine,"To him I slowly said;"You trampled on the dead of mineAnd told me they are dead."

[Pg 68]
HIS OTHER CHANCE

He was down and out, and his pluck was gone,And he said to me in a gloomy way:"I've wasted my chances, one by one,And I'm just no good, as the people say.Nothing ahead, and my dreams all dust,Though once there was something I might have been,But I wasn't game, and I broke my trust,And I wasn't straight and I wasn't clean."

"You're pretty low down," says I to him,"But nobody's holding you there, my friend.Life is a stream where men sink or swim,And the drifters come to a sorry end;But there's two of you living and breathing still—The fellow you are, and he's tough to see,And another chap, if you've got the will,The man that you still have a chance to be."

He laughed with scorn. "Is there two of me?I thought I'd murdered the other one.I once knew a chap that I hoped to be,And he was decent, but now he's gone.""Well," says I, "it may seem to youThat life has little of joy in store,But there's always something you still can do,And there's never a man but can try once more.

"His Other Chance"
From a drawing by **W. T. BENDA.**

[Pg 69]
"There are always two to the end of time—The fellow we are and the future man.The Lord never meant you should cease to climb,And you can get up if you think you can.The fellow you are is a sorry sight,But you needn't go drifting out to sea.Get hold of yourself and travel right;There's a fellow you've still got a chance to be."

[Pg 70]
THE FAMILY DOCTOR

I've tried the high-toned specialists, who doctor folks to-day;I've heard the throat man whisper low "Come on now let us spray";I've sat in fancy offices and waited long my turn,And paid for fifteen minutes what it took a week to earn;But while these scientific men are kindly, one and all,I miss the good old doctor that my mother used to call.

The old-time family doctor! Oh, I am sorry that he's gone,He ushered us into the world and knew us every one;He didn't have to ask a lot of questions, for he knewOur histories from birth and all the ailments we'd been through.And though as children small we feared the medicines he'd send,The old-time family doctor grew to be our dearest friend.

No hour too late, no night too rough for him to heed our call;He knew exactly where to hang his coat up in the hall;He knew exactly where to go, which room upstairs to find[Pg 71]The patient he'd been called to see, and saying: "Never mind,I'll run up there myself and see what's causing all the fuss."It seems we grew to look and lean on him as one of us.

He had a big and kindly heart, a fine and tender way,And more than once I've wished that I could call him in to-day.The specialists are clever men and busy men, I know,And haven't time to doctor as they did long years ago;But some day he may come again, the friend that we can call,The good old family doctor who will love us one and all.

[Pg 72]

DENIAL

I'd like to give 'em all they ask—it hurts to have to answer, "No,"And say they cannot have the things they tell me they are wanting so;Yet now and then they plead for what I know would not be good to giveOr what I can't afford to buy, and that's the hardest hour I live.

They little know or understand how happy I would be to grantTheir every wish, yet there are times it isn't wise, or else I can't.And sometimes, too, I can't explain the reason when they question whyTheir pleadings for some passing joy it is my duty to deny.

I only know I'd like to see them smile forever on life's way;I would not have them shed one tear or ever meet a troubled day.And I would be content with life and gladly face each dreary task,If I could always give to them the little treasures that they ask.

"Denial"
From a painting by **F. C. YOHN.**

[Pg 73]

Sometimes we pray to God above and ask for joys that are denied,And when He seems to scorn our plea, in bitterness we turn aside.And yet the Father of us all, Who sees and knows just what is best,May wish, as often here we wish, that He could grant what we request.

[Pg 74]

THE WORKMAN'S DREAM

To-day it's dirt and dust and steam,To-morrow it will be the same,And through it all the soul must dreamAnd try to play a manly game;Dirt, dust and steam and harsh commands,Yet many a soft hand passes byAnd only thinks he understandsThe purpose of my task and why.

I've seen men shudder just to seeMe standing at this lathe of mine,And knew somehow they pitied me,But I have never made a whine;For out of all this dirt and dustAnd clang and clamor day by day,Beyond toil's everlasting "must,"I see my little ones at play.

The hissing steam would drive me madIf hissing steam was all I heard;But there's a boy who calls me dadWho daily keeps my courage spurred;And there's a little girl who waitsEach night for all that I may bring,And I'm the guardian of their fates,Which makes this job a wholesome thing.[Pg 75]

Beyond the dust and dirt and steamI see a college where he'll go;And when I shall fulfill my dream,More than his father he will know;And she shall be a woman fair,Fit for the world to love and trust—I'll give my land a glorious pairOut of this place of dirt and dust.

[Pg 76]
THE HOMELY MAN

Looks as though a cyclone hit him—Can't buy clothes that seem to fit him;An' his cheeks are rough like leather,Made for standin' any weather.Outwards he wuz fashioned plainly,Loose o' joint an' blamed ungainly,But I'd give a lot if I'dBeen prepared so fine inside.

Best thing I can tell you of himIs the way the children love him.Now an' then I get to thinkin'He is much like old Abe Lincoln—Homely like a gargoyle graven,An' looks worse when he's unshaven;But I'd take his ugly phizJes' to have a heart like his.

I ain't over-sentimental,But old Blake is so blamed gentleAn' so thoughtful-like of othersHe reminds us of our mothers.Rough roads he is always smoothin',An' his way is, oh, so soothin'That he takes away the stingWhen your heart is sorrowing.

"The Homely Man"
From a painting by **M. L. BOWER.**

[Pg 77]
Children gather round about himLike they can't get on without him.An' the old depend upon him,Pilin' all their burdens on him,Like as though the thing that grieves 'emHas been lifted when he leaves 'em.Homely? That can't be denied.But he's glorious inside.

[Pg 78]
UNCHANGEABLE MOTHER

Mothers never change, I guess,In their tender thoughtfulness.Makes no difference that you growUp to forty years or so,Once you cough, you'll find that sheSees you as you used to be,An' she wants to tell to youAll the things that you must do.

Just show symptoms of a cold,She'll forget that you've grown old.Though there's silver in your hair,Still you need a mother's care,An' she'll ask you things like these:"You still wearing b. v. d.'s?Summer days have long since gone,You should have your flannels on."

Grown and married an' maybeFather of a family,But to mother you are stillJust her boy when you are ill;Just the lad that used to needPlasters made of mustard seed;An' she thinks she has to seeThat you get your flaxseed tea.[Pg 79]

Mothers never change, I guess,In their tender thoughtfulness.All her gentle long life throughShe is bent on nursing you;An' although you may be grown,She still claims you for her own,An' to her you'll always beJust a youngster at her knee.

[Pg 80]
LIFE

Life is a jest;Take the delight of it.Laughter is best;Sing through the night of it.Swiftly the tearAnd the hurt and the ache of itFind us down here;Life must be what we make of it.

Life is a song;Let us dance to the thrill of it.Grief's hours are long,And cold is the chill of it.Joy is man's need;Let us smile for the sake of it.This be our creed:Life must be what we make of it.

Life is a soul;The virtue and vice of it.Strife for a goal,And man's strength is the price of it.Your life and mine,The bare bread and the cake of it,End in this line:Life must be what we make of it.

"Life"
From a charcoal drawing by **W. T. BENDA.**

[Pg 81]

SUCCESS

This I would claim for my success—not fame nor gold,Nor the throng's changing cheers from day to day,Not always ease and fortune's glad display,Though all of these are pleasant joys to hold;But I would like to have my story toldBy smiling friends with whom I've shared the way,Who, thinking of me, nod their heads and say:"His heart was warm when other hearts were cold.

"None turned to him for aid and found it not,His eyes were never blind to man's distress,Youth and old age he lived, nor once forgotThe anguish and the ache of loneliness;His name was free from stain or shameful blotAnd in his friendship men found happiness."

[Pg 82]

THE LONELY OLD FELLOW

The roses are bedded for winter, the tulips are planted for spring;The robins and martins have left us; there are only the sparrows to sing.The garden seems solemnly silent, awaiting its blankets of snow,And I feel like a lonely old fellow with nowhere to turn or to go.

All summer I've hovered about them, all summer they've nodded at me;I've wandered and waited among them the first pink of blossom to see;I've known them and loved and caressed them, and now all their splendor has fled,And the harsh winds of winter all tell me the friends of my garden are dead.

I'm a lonely old fellow, that's certain. All winter with nothing to doBut sit by the window recalling the days when my skies were all blue;But my heart is not given to sorrow and never my lips shall complain,For winter shall pass and the sunshine shall give me my roses again.[Pg 83]

And so for the friends that have vanished, the friends that they tell me are dead,Who have traveled the road to God's Acres and sleep where the willows are spread;They have left me a lonely old fellow to sit here and dream by the pane,But I know, like the friends of my garden, we shall all meet together again.

[Pg 84]
SOMEBODY ELSE

Somebody wants a new bonnet to wear;Somebody wants a new dress;Somebody needs a new bow for her hair,And never the wanting grows less.Oh, this is the reason I labor each dayAnd this is the joy of my tasks:That deep in the envelope holding my payIs something that somebody asks.

I could go begging for water and breadAnd travel the highways of ease,But somebody wants a roof over his headAnd stockings to cover his knees.I could go shirking the duties of lifeAnd laugh when necessity pleads,But rather I stand to the toil and the strifeTo furnish what somebody needs.

Somebody wants what I've strength to supply,And somebody's waiting for meTo come home to-night with money to buyHer bread and her cake and her tea.And as I am strong so her laughter will ring,And as I am true she will smile;It's the somebody else of the toiler or kingThat makes all the struggle worth while.

"Somebody Else"
From a charcoal drawing by M. L. BOWER.

[Pg 85]
Somebody needs all the courage I own,And somebody's trust is in me;For never a man who can go it alone,Whatever his station may be.So I stand to my task and I stand to my care,And struggle to come to success,For the ribbons to tie up somebody's hair,And my somebody's pretty new dress.

[Pg 86]
EFFORT

He brought me his report card from the teacher and he saidHe wasn't very proud of it and sadly bowed his head.He was excellent in reading, but arithmetic, was fair,And I noticed there were several "unsatisfactorys" there;But one little bit of credit which was given brought me joy—He was "excellent in effort," and I fairly hugged the boy.

"Oh, it doesn't make much difference what is written on your card,"I told that little fellow, "if you're only trying hard.The 'very goods' and 'excellents' are fine, I must agree,But the effort you are making means a whole lot more to me;And the thing that's most important when this card is put asideIs to know, in spite of failure, that to do your best you've tried.

"Just keep excellent in effort—all the rest will come to you.There isn't any problem but some day you'll learn to do,[Pg 87]And at last, when you grow older, you will come to understandThat by hard and patient toiling men have risen to commandAnd some day you will discover when a greater goal's at stakeThat better far than brilliance is the effort you will make."

[Pg 88]
LIVING

The miser thinks he's living when he's hoarding up his gold;The soldier calls it living when he's doing something bold;The sailor thinks it living to be tossed upon the sea,And upon this very subject no two men of us agree.But I hold to the opinion, as I walk my way along,That living's made of laughter and good-fellowship and song.

I wouldn't call it living to be always seeking gold,To bank all the present gladness for the days when I'll be old.I wouldn't call it living to spend all my strength for fame,And forego the many pleasures which to-day are mine to claim.I wouldn't for the splendor of the world set out to roam,And forsake my laughing children and the peace I know at home.

"Living"
From a painting by **FRANK X. LEYENDECKER.**

Oh, the thing that I call living isn't gold or fame at all!It's fellowship and sunshine, and it's roses by the wall.It's evenings glad with music and a hearth-fire that's ablaze,[Pg 89]And the joys which come to mortals in a thousand different ways.It is laughter and contentment and the struggle for a goal;It is everything that's needful in the shaping of a soul.

[Pg 90]
A WARM HOUSE
AND A RUDDY FIRE

A warm house and a ruddy fire,To what more can man aspire?Eyes that shine with love aglow,Is there more for man to know?

Whether home be rich or poor,If contentment mark the doorHe who finds it good to liveHas the best that life can give.

This the end of mortal strife!Peace at night to sweeten life,Rest when mind and body tire,At contentment's ruddy fire.

Rooms where merry songs are sung,Happy old and glorious young;These, if perfect peace be known,Both the rich and poor must own.

A warm house and a ruddy fire,These the goals of all desire,These the dream of every manSince God spoke and life began.

[Pg 91]
THE ONE IN TEN

Nine passed him by with a hasty look,Each bent on his eager way;One glance at him was the most they took,"Somebody stuck," said they;But it never occurred to the nine to heedA stranger's plight and a stranger's need.

The tenth man looked at the stranded car,And he promptly stopped his own."Let's see if I know what your troubles are,"Said he in a cheerful tone;"Just stuck in the mire. Here's a cable stout,Hitch onto my bus and I'll pull you out."

"A thousand thanks," said the stranger then,"For the debt that I owe you;I've counted them all and you're one in tenSuch a kindly deed to do."And the tenth man smiled and he answered then,"Make sure that you'll be the one in ten."

Are you one of the nine who pass men byIn this hasty life we live?Do you refuse with a downcast eyeThe help which you could give?Or are you the one in ten whose creedIs always to stop for the man in need?

[Pg 92]

TO A YOUNG MAN

The great were once as you.They whom men magnify to-dayOnce groped and blundered on life's way,Were fearful of themselves, and thoughtBy magic was men's greatness wrought.They feared to try what they could do;Yet Fame hath crowned with her successThe selfsame gifts that you possess.

The great were young as you,Dreaming the very dreams you hold,Longing yet fearing to be bold,Doubting that they themselves possessedThe strength and skill for every test,Uncertain of the truths they knew,Not sure that they could stand to fateWith all the courage of the great.

Then came a day when theyTheir first bold venture made,Scorning to cry for aid.They dared to stand to fight alone,Took up the gauntlet life had thrown,Charged full-front to the fray,Mastered their fear of self, and then,Learned that our great men are but men.

"To A Young Man"
From a charcoal drawing by **W. T. BENDA.**

[Pg 93]

Oh, youth, go forth and do!You, too, to fame may rise;You can be strong and wise.Stand up to life and play the man—You can if you'll but think you can;The great were once as you.You envy them their proud success?'Twas won with gifts that you possess.

[Pg 94]

AFRAID OF HIS DAD

Bill Jones, who goes to school with me,Is the saddest boy I ever see.He's just so 'fraid he runs awayWhen all of us fellows want to play,An' says he dassent stay aboutCoz if his father found it outHe'd wallop him. An' he can't goWith us to see a picture showOn Saturdays, an' it's too bad,But he's afraid to ask his dad.

When he gets his report card, heIs just as scared as scared can be,An' once I saw him when he criedBecoz although he'd tried an' triedHis best, the teacher didn't careAn' only

24

marked his spelling fair,An' he told me there'd be a fightWhen his dad saw his card that night.It seems to me it's awful badTo be so frightened of your dad.

My Dad ain't that way—I can goAn' tell him everything I know,An' ask him things, an' when he comesBack home at night he says we're chums;An' we go out an' take a walk,[Pg 95]An' all the time he lets me talk.I ain't scared to tell him whatI've done to-day that I should not;When I get home I'm always gladTo stay around an' play with Dad.

Bill Jones, he says, he wishes heCould have a father just like me,But his dad hasn't time to play,An' so he chases him awayAn' scolds him when he makes a noiseAn' licks him if he breaks his toys.Sometimes Bill says he's got to lieOr else get whipped, an' that is whyIt seems to me it's awful badTo be so frightened of your dad.

[Pg 96]
SERVICE

I have no wealth of gold to give away,But I can pledge to worthy causes these:I'll give my strength, my days and hours of ease,My finest thought and courage when I may,And take some deed accomplished for my pay.I cannot offer much in silver fees,But I can serve when richer persons play,And with my presence fill some vacancies.

There are some things beyond the gift of gold,A richer treasure's needed now and then;Some joys life needs which are not bought and sold—The high occasion often calls for men.Some for release from service give their pelf,But he gives most who freely gives himself.

Printed in Great Britain
by Amazon